The Colony of Maryland

A Primary Source History

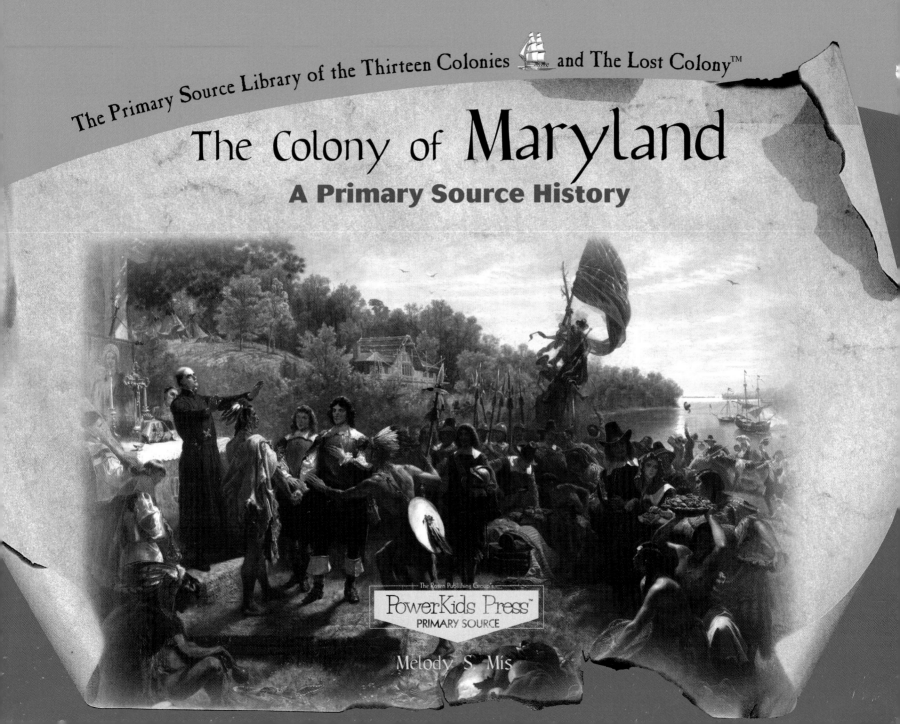

The Rosen Publishing Group's

PowerKids Press™

PRIMARY SOURCE

Melody S. Mis

To Former Marylanders Bob and Cheryl Senn

Published in 2007 by The Rosen Publishing Group, Inc.
29 East 21st Street, New York, NY 10010

First Edition

Editor: Jennifer Way
Book Design: Ginny Chu
Layout Design: Julio A. Gil
Photo Researcher: Marty Levick

Photo Credits: Cover, p. 16 (inset) The Maryland Historical Society, Baltimore, Maryland; p. 4 The New York Public Library/Art Resource, NY; pp. 4 (inset), 14 (inset) Bridgeman Art Library; pp. 6, 8 Historic St. Mary's City; pp. 6 (inset), 8 (inset), 10 (inset), 16, 18 (inset), 20 Collection of the Maryland State Archives; p. 10 © New-York Historical Society, New York, USA/Bridgeman Art Library; pp. 12, 14 Getty Images; p. 12 (inset) British Library, London, Great Britain/HIP/Art Resouce, NY; p. 18 © North Wind Picture Archives; p. 20 (inset) photograph courtesy Peabody Essex Museum.

Library of Congress Cataloging-in-Publication Data

Mis, Melody S.
    The colony of Maryland : a primary source history / Melody S. Mis.— 1st ed.
        p. cm. — (The primary source library of the thirteen colonies and the Lost Colony)
    Includes index.
    ISBN 1-4042-3434-9 (library binding)
    1. Maryland—History—Colonial period, ca. 1600–1775—Juvenile literature. 2. Maryland—History—1775–1865—Juvenile literature. 3. Maryland—History—Colonial period, ca. 1600–1775—Sources—Juvenile literature. 4. Maryland—History—1775–1865—Sources—Juvenile literature. I. Title. II. Series.
    F184.M67 2007
    975.2'02—dc22

                                    2005025626

Manufactured in the United States of America

Contents

A New Map of
VIRGINIA
and
MARYLAND
By Robt. Morden

B. Baltimore C
A. Arundelton C
Cal. Calverton C
Ch. Charles C
M Mary C
Cæ Cæcil C
F Talbot C
D Dorchester C
K Kent C
We Westmorland
No Northumberland
La Lancester
Mi Middlesex
Gl Glacester
C Charles C
Y York C
W Warwick
E Elizabeth
LN Lower Norfolk
Na Nantimond
Co Corratuck
N Northampton
Ac Accomaco
Ar Arcadia

Maryland is on the Chesapeake Bay, as can be seen in this 1680 map. The Chesapeake Bay is an estuary, which is a place where the freshwater of a river meets the salt water of an ocean. Inset: This painting of John Smith was made around 1616. He was the first European to explore the Chesapeake Bay area.

Discovering Maryland's Chesapeake Bay

Maryland was the fourth American colony to be founded. However, Maryland was already **inhabited** by the Yaocomaco Native Americans.

One of the first Europeans to see Maryland was the Italian **explorer** Giovanni da Verrazano. In 1524, he sailed to Chincoteague Bay. The first European to set foot in Maryland was the Englishman John Smith. In 1608, he explored the Chesapeake Bay area. Soon English traders began visiting Maryland to trade with the Native Americans. In 1631, Englishman William Claiborne built a trading post on Kent Island. This is often thought of as the first English settlement in Maryland.

The Yaocomaco lived in houses called *witchotts*. They built their *witchotts* out of tree trunks, then covered the outsides with grass mats. About 10 people could live in each *witchott*. A Yaocomaco village was often made up of 15 or more *witchotts*. They were placed in a circle and surrounded by a wooden fence for security.

Saint Mary's City, shown here, was founded in 1634. It was Maryland's capital until 1694, when it was moved to Annapolis. Inset: In 1632, King Charles I granted a proprietary charter to the Calvert family. A proprietary charter granted land to one or more people. These people could rent or sell parts of the land. They also made laws for the colony and appointed a governor.

Lord Baltimore Founds Maryland

In 1625, England's king, James I, gave George Calvert the title Lord Baltimore. Calvert wanted to establish a colony where people could practice their religion freely. At that time the English did not grant many rights to people who did not belong to the country's official church, the Church of England.

In 1632, England's king, Charles I, granted the Calvert family a **proprietary charter** for a colony. Calvert named this colony Maryland. When George Calvert died, his son Cecil became the second Lord Baltimore. In 1633, Cecil appointed his brother Leonard to lead settlers to Maryland. In 1634, they founded Maryland's first colony, Saint Mary's City.

Many colonists came to Maryland as indentured servants. An indentured servant was someone who promised to work for four or more years for anyone who paid his or her way to America. After this period the person would be freed and given clothing, a gun to use for hunting food, and a small piece of land.

This Yaocomaco witchott has been rebuilt near Saint Mary's City. Inset: Leonard Calvert led the ships the Ark and the Dove from England to Maryland in 1633. He was Maryland's first governor, holding the position until his death in 1647.

Settling Maryland

When the settlers arrived at Saint Mary's City, they met the Yaocomaco. The Yaocomaco were ready to move to another place, because they no longer got along with the nearby Susquehannock. The Yaocomaco sold their village to the colonists for tools and cloth.

Lord Baltimore controlled the colony and made its laws. He rented land to colonists and collected taxes on goods that were shipped to the colony from other countries. The colonists were allowed to have an **assembly**, but they could not make laws for the colony. This often caused problems between the colonists and Lord Baltimore. The colonists believed they should have a voice in their government, as the people in Britain had in theirs.

Maryland's religious acceptance led groups such as the Puritans to move to the colony. Inset: The Act Concerning Religion punished people who openly spoke against others' beliefs. The Catholic Calvert family wanted Maryland colonists to be able to practice religion freely, because the Calverts had been punished for their beliefs in England.

Maryland's Early Years

During the colony's first 10 years, sickness killed one of every five people. People continued to move there, however, hoping to make money in business or farming. Others came for religious freedom. In 1649, Lord Baltimore passed a historic law called the Act Concerning Religion. This act granted religious freedom to Marylanders.

After the law was passed, **Puritans** moved to Maryland. They established the town of Annapolis and began to take part in Maryland's government. By 1654, the Puritans had gained so much power in the colony's government that they took over and did away with the Act Concerning Religion. The act was reestablished four years later. In 1658, the British leader Oliver Cromwell returned the control of Maryland to Lord Baltimore.

Mr. MOALE'S View of BALTIMORE in 1752.

Population *about* 300 Persons.

Tonnage 1 *Brig* 122 *Tons burthen*.

Baltimore was an important port for shipping the tobacco grown in Maryland. The tobacco trade grew when slaves began to be used in the colony. Slavery had been lawful in Maryland since 1664. By the beginning of the American Revolution, slaves would make up about one-third of Maryland's population. Inset: William and Mary's rule lasted from 1689 until 1702, when William died. Mary had died in 1694.

ATLAN

Tobacco and Slavery in Maryland

In 1689, England's rulers, King William and Queen Mary, made Maryland a royal colony. This meant Maryland would be under the control of the king and queen.

People continued to move to Maryland, hoping to get rich from raising tobacco. It was a growing business in the colonies. The problem with raising tobacco was that it required a lot of labor. It was hard for farmers to be able to pay workers and still make money, so they began to use slaves. By the mid-1700s, Maryland had grown. New towns had been founded, including Baltimore. In 1767, Pennsylvania and Maryland settled a disagreement over their border. Charles Mason and Jeremiah Dixon had **surveyed** the area and marked the line between the two colonies.

The French and Indian War was fought between 1754 and 1763. The French and the British were fighting over land in the North American colonies. Inset: This painting of George III was made around the time he became king, in 1760.

Britain's Unfair Taxes on the Colonies

By the mid-1700s, the 13 colonies were beginning to object to Britain's laws and taxes. After Britain won the French and Indian War in 1763, it needed to pay for it. Since the fighting had occurred in the colonies, Britain decided they should pay for the war through taxes. The Stamp Act of 1765 said that the colonists had to buy a stamp for paper goods. Marylanders refused to buy the stamps and closed all the public offices on the day the Stamp Act was to begin. Britain **repealed** the unpopular act in 1766, although Britain continued to pass taxes that angered the colonists.

The colonists were also angry because they were not **represented** in the British government, which was passing these laws. They called it "taxation without representation."

From a Continental Association Broadside

"The whole Continent from Nova-Scotia to Georgia have by their Delegates come into Measures, which if adhered to, will I trust, frustrate every Scheme of Administration to deprive you of your invaluable Privileges."

This broadside explains that the colonies have decided to boycott British goods in an effort to make Britain treat the colonies more fairly. It goes on to state that Colonial businesses should not use the lack of goods to raise their prices.

In 1774, Anthony Stewart burned his ship, the Peggy Stewart, because he feared what Maryland patriots would do if they found out he had gone against the boycott of British goods. To boycott means to refuse to buy something. Inset: The Continental Association made sure that colonists boycotted British goods. This 1774 broadside explains the purpose of the boycotts.

Maryland Objects to Taxation

In 1774, Marylanders Samuel Chase, Robert Goldsborough, Thomas Johnson, William Paca, and Matthew Tilghman met with Colonial leaders in Philadelphia, Pennsylvania, to talk about Britain's unfair taxes. This was the First Continental Congress.

In the meantime **patriots** in Maryland joined the Continental Association. The Continental Association's purpose was to hurt British businesses by refusing to buy goods from them.

The British paid no attention to the colonists' actions. In April 1775, British soldiers fought with Colonial soldiers at Lexington, Massachusetts. This battle started the **American Revolution**.

In October 1774, Anthony Stewart sailed his ship, called the *Peggy Stewart*, into Annapolis. He had bought a lot of tea in Britain and planned to pay the tax on it and then sell it. This act angered Maryland patriots because it was against the 1774 decision of the colonists not to buy British goods. Stewart was afraid of the patriots, so he burned his own ship and the tea on it.

The Second Continental Congress created the Continental army and made George Washington, shown here, the army's leader. Inset: Charles Carroll served on the Second Continental Congress and signed the Declaration of Independence. After the war he served in Maryland's senate and in the U.S. Senate.

Maryland Declares Independence from Britain

In May 1775, leaders of the colonies met in Philadelphia, Pennsylvania, to talk about the war. This meeting was called the Second Continental Congress. Maryland sent William Paca, Thomas Stone, Samuel Chase, and Charles Carroll. Congress decided that if the colonies **united** against the British, they would have a better chance of winning independence.

Congress asked each colony to bring together troops to form the Continental army. Then Congress voted on whether the colonies wanted to be free of British rule. On July 4, 1776, the colonies wrote the **Declaration of Independence** which said they were free from Britain. Charles Carroll, Samuel Chase, William Paca, and Thomas Stone signed the declaration for Maryland. The colonies had declared their independence. Then they had to fight to win it.

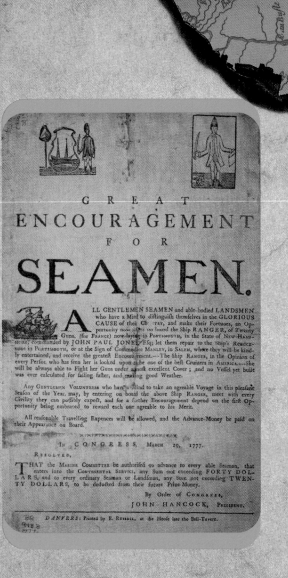

This 1784 painting shows George Washington, General Lafayette, and Tench Tilghman, of Maryland, at Yorktown, Virginia. Tilghman worked closely with Washington throughout the war. Inset: This broadside asks patriots who have boats or who know how to sail ships to become privateers.

Maryland During the American Revolution

Only a few battles were fought in Maryland during the Revolution. However, Maryland was one of the first colonies to provide troops for the Continental army. General George Washington called Maryland soldiers "troops of the line." This earned Maryland the nickname the "Old Line State."

Maryland also helped the war effort by providing about 250 privateers. Privateers were people who owned trading ships. During the war Congress allowed the privateers to take British ships and to keep whatever the ships were carrying. This kept supplies from reaching British soldiers.

The Revolution ended in 1781, when the Continental army won at Yorktown, Virginia. Marylanders Tench Tilghman went to Philadelphia to tell Congress that the Americans had won the war.

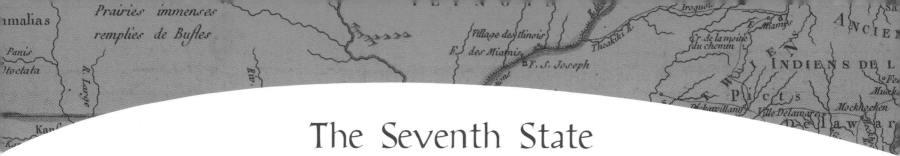

The Seventh State

In 1783, the war officially came to an end. Now the newly formed United States needed to set up a government. During the war they had followed the Articles of Confederation. The articles did not provide for a president, a capital, or a national government that gave the states a way to work together as a country.

In May 1787, the Constitutional Convention was held in Philadelphia. Maryland sent James McHenry, Daniel Carroll, Daniel of St. Thomas Jenifer, Luther Martin, and John Mercer. After the representatives had written the **Constitution**, Jenifer, McHenry, and Carroll signed it. Martin and Mercer did not. On April 28, 1788, Maryland adopted the Constitution and became the seventh state to join the United States. In 1791, Maryland gave some of its land to the government for a capital, which became Washington, D.C.

Glossary

American Revolution (uh-MER-uh-ken reh-vuh-LOO-shun) Battles that soldiers from the colonies fought against Britain for freedom, from 1775 to 1783.

assembly (uh-SEM-blee) A group of people who meet to advise a government.

Constitution (kon-stih-TOO-shun) The basic rules by which the United States is governed.

Declaration of Independence (deh-kluh-RAY-shun UV in-duh-PEN-dints) An official announcement signed on July 4, 1776, in which American colonists stated they were free of British rule.

explorer (ek-SPLOR-ur) A person who travels and looks for new land.

inhabited (in-HA-but-ed) Lived in.

patriots (PAY-tree-uts) American colonists who believed in separating from British rule.

proprietary charter (pruh-PRY-uh-ter-ee CHAR-tur) An official agreement giving someone permission to start a privately owned colony or settlement.

Puritans (PYUR-ih-tenz) Members of a religious group in England who moved to America during the seventeenth century.

repealed (rih-PEELD) Did away with.

represented (rih-prih-ZENT-ed) Stood for.

surveyed (ser-VAYD) Measured land.

united (yoo-NYT-ed) Joined together to act as a single group.

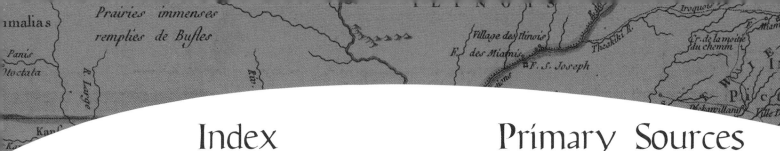

Index

Primary Sources

Page 4. A new map of Virginia and Maryland. 1680, Art Resource, The New York Public Library, New York. **Page 4. Inset.** Captain John Smith, 1st Governor of Virginia. Oil on canvas, circa 1616, English School, Bridgeman Art Library, Private Collection. **Page 6. Inset.** The Charter of Maryland. June 20, 1632, Collection of the Maryland State Archives, Annapolis, Maryland. **Page 10. Inset.** An Act Concerning Religion. April 21, 1649, Collection of the Maryland State Archives, Annapolis, Maryland. **Page 12. Inset.** Portrait of William and Mary. Circa 18th century, British Library, London, Great Britain/HIP/Art Resource, NY, British Library, London, United Kingdom. **Page 14. Inset.** Portrait of George III in his Coronation Robes. Oil on canvas, circa 1760, Allan Ramsay, Bridgeman Art Library, Private Collection. **Page 16. Inset.** Continental Association Broadside. November 11, 1774, A Mechanic, The Maryland Historical Society, Baltimore, Maryland. **Page 20.** Washington, Lafayette, and Tilghman at Yorktown. Oil on canvas, 1784, Charles Willson Peale, Collection of the Maryland State Archives, Maryland State House, Old Senate Chamber, Annapolis, Maryland. **Page 20. Inset.** Great Encouragement for Seamen. Broadside, photograph courtesy Peabody Essex Museum, Salem, Massachusetts.

Web Sites

Due to the changing nature of Internet links, PowerKids Press has developed an online list of Web sites related to the subject of this book. This site is updated regularly. Please use this link to access the list: www.powerkidslinks.com/lotc/maryland/